Gypsy the Goat

Vern Miller

Illustrated by Marsha Stanley

Copyright © 2013, by Vern Miller
Gypsy the Goat
Vern Miller
www.sgtimberframe.com
vern@sgtimberframe.com

Illustrated by Marsha Cates Stanley

Published 2013, by Light Messages
www.lightmessages.com
Durham, NC 27713
Printed in the United States of America
ISBN: 978-1-61153-082-7

To my wife Tina and my daughter Christa. Over the years I think the three of us have made a pretty good family team. Though we have never had a goat we have had several Gypsys.

Gypsy the Goat

The far away look in Gypsy's eyes was neither angry nor sad - more like a disappointed, but determined look. Gypsy wore the same wide, brown leather collar that he always wore. But now there was a chain attached - the kind sometimes used to tie the milk cow to a tree while she would graze in different places around the farm. The other end was attached to the post that held up the barn-shed roof.

Bart, the Bluebird, was above, on a limb, which was growing from the huge oak tree in the barnyard. "Gypsy," Bart said, "are you tied up again?" Gypsy rolled his gaze up at Bart, then back out as before with nary a motion, except to rearrange the wad of hay he was chewing on. Gypsy knew that he was leaving today, but he did not know where the people were taking him. Gypsy loved the countryside; and he loved the free, roaming life, not having a home. But until now, he had not bothered to think about all the problems he had caused; with disregard being his nature.

This small farm was Bart's home, and it had been for quite some time. His nest was in the rafters on the other side of the barn, and the fields around were his dining room with plenty of bugs and insects to eat. Bart was there when Gypsy first arrived and he knew the whole story.

Chapter One

Christa woke one fine spring morning, stretched, and looked out her bedroom window, as she usually did. Most of the the time there were squirrels chasing each other up and down the big oak tree. Sometimes early, on misty, foggy mornings, there would be deer grazing in the large field behind her home. Christa lived with her mom and dad in a big yellow house, on a small farm. It was just outside of town on North Road, but Christa still could easily walk or ride her bike to the store down on Riverfront Street.

This certain morning, what Christa saw out her window, while resembling a deer in shape and size, was surely not a deer at all. "Mom, Dad," Christa called, "Look at what's out in the field!"

The shaggy animal they saw had large curved horns and a beard.

"It's someone's goat," Mom said.

"That's Gypsy!" exclaimed Dad.

Everyone around had heard of Gypsy at one time or another. He had been roaming the countryside, around these parts, for a number of years.

"What is that goat doing in our field?" Mom asked Dad.

"I don't know; he must be on the loose again," Dad replied.

They all walked out the back door toward the field, not quite sure what to do. Gypsy had a reputation around town for causing spurts of mischief, but they had not heard of him hurting anyone.

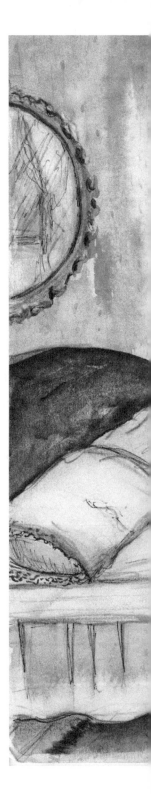

He had never had a long-term owner; he would always find a way to get out of someone's fence, or a chance to sneak off, or he would just plain wear out his welcome, which tended to be the majority of the time.

Dad slowed down long enough to grab an old rope hanging from the shed. As they approached, Gypsy seemed to not even notice them. He turned to look; then he went back to nibbling the young grass he had spotted from down the road.

"We will find out who has been keeping him and take him back this evening," Dad said as he tied the goat to the barn. "I don't want this goat causing problems around here," he added.

Christa started growing fond of Gypsy right away. He didn't smell great, but he was kind of handsome-looking in a rugged sort of way.

"What if we can't find his owner; what will we do then Dad?" asked Christa. She already liked the idea of having a goat around.

"We'll worry about that when the time comes," her father replied, "but now I have to go to work, and that goat has already caused me to be late.

Chapter Two

Christa's dad had a business across town, on the river, where he loaded and unloaded the small freight ships that came in. He stored some of the freight and sent the rest off in trucks. Her mom stayed at home where she had her own business, making special little socks for babies. She worked in a room in the house, doing her sewing and dyeing. She sometimes would draw little pictures on the socks, and then she would send them out in the mail to people who called from all over the state. Christa had always thought that her mom was quite artistic.

When they were not at their jobs or in school, the whole family would spend a lot of time keeping the little farm on which they lived going. They had gotten it several years ago from dad's uncle. It had just sat for a long time and had gotten run down; but their work was paying off, and gradually things were shaping up.

Meanwhile, at work, Christa's father had gotten nowhere finding where Gypsy's last home was, or he was finding out that no one wanted him. When he had a few minutes, her dad walked to the barbershop and asked everyone he knew about the goat. Mr. Blanchard, who ran the hardware store, said he had seen him in Nat Willow's garden, day before yesterday.

"Or was it Saturday?" He kind of strained to recall.

Dad went over to the tire store where Nat was helping a customer. Just the mention of that goat made Nat furious.

"He ate a whole row of runners," Nat said, referring to the climbing beans he was growing. "Then he trampled half my tomato vines; why I don't care if I never see that goat again!"

"I see," replied Dad. Things were pretty much the same all over town; if anyone had anything to say about Gypsy it was nothing good.

Chapter Three

That evening at supper, Dad was telling everyone what he found out during the day. Just about that time, Mom went to the back porch to get the apple pie she had baked for dessert. She left it sitting on the table by the window to cool, but it was no longer there.

"My pie is gone!" She cried excitedly; "There's a big hole in the window screen, too."

Dad came running. When they looked outside, all they could find was an empty pie plate and some hoof tracks.

"That goat," murmured Dad, half to himself.

They looked toward the barn, but Gypsy was nowhere to be seen. A piece of the rope that was used to tie him was hanging from the post. No one had thought that a goat might eat a rope just like all those other things that a goat might eat.

They looked around the barn and around the house. They looked out back in the field and even in the small basement under the house where the door had a big hole, but there was no sign of Gypsy.

"He must have decided to take off," said Mom.

"Good; maybe we won't have to fool with him any longer," said Dad.

But Christa was sad. Though she thought her mom and dad didn't know it, she had been with Gypsy all morning. She had made sure that he had plenty of cool water to drink and some hay to eat. She even picked him some clover from the yard. Christa had thought that she and Gypsy were becoming good friends; now he had run off.

Chapter Four

Although Gypsy was a roaming goat, he was not the kind to leave a good thing right away. After all that good hay and clover, along with a piece of window screen, and a whole apple pie for dessert, he had merely turned in early. He had climbed onto the old wagon, then up through the open hay door, to the barn loft to sleep.

The next morning, Christa looked out her window, as usual. Much to her surprise, there was Gypsy, standing in the open door in the top of the barn, stretching and yawning, slow to wake up from a wonderful night's sleep. Christa ran shouting,

"Mom, Dad, Gypsy's in the top of the barn; he didn't leave after all."

Dad looked. Sure enough, that long-horned goat was up in the barn, scratching his neck on a loose board, just acting like he was at home.

"Well I'm not letting him run loose and tear up this place all day," said Dad, grabbing the chain this time, instead of a rope.

Dad struggled up the old ladder to the loft, with the chain draped around his shoulder, but Gypsy was not to be caught as easily as before. Why, with a good meal in his belly, and a good night's sleep, he was raring to go. Just as Dad grabbed his collar, Gypsy leaped across the floor with one hop, then down onto the wagon below, as effortlessly as one of his mountain goat cousins, on some rocky hillside. The only problem was, Dad had not let go of the collar. They both went through the doorway, and Dad landed on the wagon bed, below, with a thud.

Gypsy never intended to hurt anyone; he was just doing what goats do – he was off to have some fun. Christa and Mom ran up to the wagon, where Dad lay moaning, to see how badly he was hurt. Gypsy trotted off toward the woods, at the same time, looking around to see what all the commotion was about.

Dr. Simms looked Dad over from head to toe. 'There are no broken bones," he reported, after what seemed to be a very long wait; "however there are several bruises. He may be sore for a few days".

On the short drive home, they went very slow, so as not to jar Dad.

"Lucky for us that pile of hay was in the wagon, to break Dad's fall," Christa said, trying to break the cold silence that rode with them. Dad's gloomy stare showed that her efforts had failed, so she decided against another try.

"That goat needs some discipline," Dad announced out of the blue. "Yes, he needs some training; he has been allowed to have his way for too long. He won't get the best of me," Dad declared, finally being able to release all of the morning's frustrations. Mom knew well of Dad's stubborn streak. She just rolled her eyes and kept quiet, hoping that his mood would pass, quickly.

Chapter Five

Gypsy didn't come around for a couple of days, but he probably would have been flattered with all of the preparation that had been going on, in anticipation of his return. Dad had rigged a trap in one of the bottom stalls of the barn. He knew that goat would be back; it was just a matter of time. Dad tied a rope to the stall door, then threaded it through an old well bucket pulley overhead. The other end of the rope was tied to an old tractor wheel they had found in a junk pile out behind the barn. One end of another rope held the tractor wheel up on a high shelf, while the opposite end was attached to a feed bucket. Dad set the trap and let Christa try it out. Sure enough – when she moved the bucket, the tractor wheel fell and slammed the stall door closed.

"That's the neatest thing I've ever seen," Christa told her Dad.

"Yes, it ought to work well," Dad said, smiling, quite proud of himself. They reset the trap and filled the bucket with corn and oats. They poured some molasses on top, and even added a slice of mom's pie just for good measure. No goat they had ever heard of could resist a feast like that.

Gypsy came in sometime during the night. The next morning, the stall door was closed, the bucket was empty, and Gypsy was over in the corner chewing a wad of hay, which he tended to do when he was taking a break.

It was Saturday, and Dad woke Christa early.

"Let's get this over with," he announced as they sat down for breakfast. "We'll teach that goat some manners; he may be useful after all. We could tie him at different places around the fields, and he could eat the honeysuckle vines so we would not have to keep them cut down."

After breakfast dad pulled an odd looking cart and harness out from under the barn shed. He had borrowed them from Mr. Murphy, down the road. Mr. Murphy's kids had once had a pony that pulled the cart while they rode. Dad thought training Gypsy to pull the cart would be a fine bit of training for a wayward goat.

Dad took the harness into the stall. Gypsy, still perched in the corner chewing on a hay wad, reminded Christa of the old men who sat around at the store, telling stories and taking it easy. They would always have a ball of tobacco protruding from their jaws, and streaks of brown juice, running down from the corners of their mouths. Dad made Christa wait outside until he could see, "what kind of fight that goat is gonna put up."

Dad led him from the stall and hooked him to the cart, with no trouble at all. It was not until Dad had gotten halfway into the cart that Gypsy felt the urge to run. He bolted like a wild horse, and took off full speed down the driveway. Dad was hanging onto the cart, screaming at Gypsy, and trying to grab hold of the harness. At the curve in the driveway Gypsy was still running strong. The cart turned over onto its side, and Dad rolled out in a pile, down the bank and into the side ditch.

Gypsy was a ways down the road when he decided to slow up. The cart was still dragging on its side, as Gypsy ambled over to the shoulder and started to nibble some wildflowers.

While Mom was helping Dad into the car for another trip to see Dr. Simms, Christa took the chain and walked down the road to where Gypsy was munching flowers. While Gypsy stood chewing, she unbuckled the harness and hooked the chain to Gypsy's collar. She then led him back to the barn and tied him to the post.

After having no broken bones for the second time, but being twice as sore and short of temper, Dad proclaimed Gypsy to be a dangerous animal and that he would be carried off to the livestock market and sold. Christa just knew that her goat would be leaving soon. She was very sad.

Chapter Six

"Well, Gypsy, it's your own doing," Bart the blue bird, said. "If you had halfway behaved yourself, you might have ended up with a nice little home here. But oh, no, you had to be your usual hardheaded self, never thinking of anyone else. And that nice little girl – she really likes you; but now she's in her room crying because you are being sent away."

"Hey!" Gypsy returned, "The people – they don't understand me; they don't realize what I could do if I were just given the chance."

"Oh yeah," chimed Bart. "Just exactly what could you do if you were given the chance?"

"Well I tell you what I could do," Gypsy replied. "If I could get loose from this chain, I would be down at the airport right now pilot'n one of those flyin' machines, carrying passengers to far away places. Why, I probably could even fly that helicopter that takes people sightseeing up and down the River."

"What makes you think you could do all that?" asked Bart, twisting his head sideways as if he were trying hard to understand.

"Well I spent many an afternoon out at the airport this past spring," said Gypsy. "I watched the planes take off and land while I was grazing along the runway. There's nothing to it," he boasted. "I even got to know old Captain McGuire pretty well. He flew in the war, you know."

"Yes I know," answered Bart. "But isn't Captain McGuire the one who took you to graze around the airport?" he asked.

"Ahhh, yes, yes he was," answered Gypsy, then wondered out loud how Bart knew so much about his escapades.

"I know that the airport is clear across the county from here, but remember, I'm a bird. Birds get around you know and they see a lot, too. Why I was sitting right up in that walnut tree behind the hanger when Captain McGuire ran you away from the airport for eating half the wing on his old biplane."

Gypsy was shocked. He had no idea that anyone knew about that little incident.

"Well," Gypsy continued impatiently, "If I were not tied here, I just know I could captain the paddleboat down on the river front. I stayed down there all summer and watched Mr. Nelson run the ship. I could take over right now, if I could get loose."

"Yeah, well," sighed Bart, now understanding Gypsy's misguided perception. "You know, my cousin Edgar was telling me just a while back about a goat that hung around the river a lot, and how one day Mr. Nelson's wife caught him in the galley of their boat. It seems that he had eaten all of their fruit, and made a big mess of the whole place. She ran him off, screaming and throwing pans. Caused a pretty big commotion I understand. You remember that, Gypsy?"

Gypsy was even more distraught. Indeed, he had built a reputation around, and a bad one at that.

"And how about Mrs. Albright's laundry? Just the other week, you ate her red checkered dress right off the clothes line, and then strewed the rest of her wash across the back yard."

"Well I was just playin'," said Gypsy, meagerly trying to defend himself.

"And what about the Mitchell's tractor?" Bart went on, almost nonstop. "You chewed up all the wires on the engine. Mr. Mitchell spent almost all day just getting it to run again."

Gypsy was getting the point all right. He had not even realized what problems his antics had caused.

Well, none of this really mattered now, because he was going away. And for the first time in a long time, Gypsy was very sad. Bart knew it, too. Bart watched as a single tear ran down Gypsy's face, and dropped from his scruffy beard.

Chapter Seven

But Bart was not telling everything that he knew. After Dad had gotten back from the doctor and calmed down somewhat, Bart had glided over to, and perched on the little cherry tree by the kitchen window. He had listened in as Christa begged her dad to give Gypsy one more chance.

"I can work with him, dad; I know I can." She pleaded. "He's not all bad, Gypsy likes me; he can be taught to behave, I know he can."

Now it was mom's turn. She had been pretty quiet about the whole affair until now. But she had noticed how much Christa liked going out to the barn to visit Gypsy. She also knew that Christa would sometimes sneak out of the house at night, to take Gypsy some treats from supper.

"I think Gypsy should get one more chance, too" she declared. "I saw how you led him back from the road after he turned the cart over, and I believe you can make something out of that ornery old goat, if you work at it."

Well after Mom spoke, that was that. Gypsy got one more chance. By that time, and after talking to Bart, he had pretty much decided to calm down some anyway.

"Surly staying here with a pretty little girl to feed me, and brush me down, is better than moving to some far-off unknown place," he thought.

Besides Gypsy wasn't getting any younger, and he really didn't mind pulling that funny little cart around, once in awhile.

Christa worked with Gypsy every day. In the evening, she fed him and brushed the cockleburs from his hair. At times she would tie him at the edge of the field. Gypsy did a wonderful job of cleaning up all the bushes and vines.

Chapter Eight

One evening after supper, everyone was relaxing. It had been a long day. Mom and Christa were in the porch swing. Dad was sitting on the steps, leaning back against the brick column. Gypsy was lying under the shed, doing his usual chewing thing, and Bart sat on a limb just above the porch roof, with a craw full of late evening insects.

Suddenly Mom said, "You know, I've been thinking. We ought to enter Gypsy in the Fourth of July parade in town. It's coming up next week. We could decorate him and his cart, and make a nice little dress for Christa. Who knows – might even win a ribbon."

Christa thought that was a wonderful idea. It took a little more convincing Dad, but he finally gave in.

The cart had been cleaned and painted by parade day. Gypsy got a bath and a good combing. All the cockleburs were gone, and he even smelled some better. Christa wore a bright red dress that her mom made just for the parade. Gypsy, and his cart, had red, white, and blue ribbons all over them. He even had a ribbon braided into his beard. And Dad had stuck a big American flag, on the cart, so it would wave behind. They not only won a ribbon but at the starting place, where the judging was done, Christa and Gypsy also got the first place trophy for being the best entry.

Most of the people, who knew Gypsy from before, didn't even recognize him now. Those who did, couldn't believe what they were seeing: a changed goat for sure, and halfway presentable, too.

Well everything so far was going along fine. The parade was almost over, and Gypsy was on his best behavior. For once he was thinking about the future, and how nice his new home was, and how much he liked his new friends.

Everything was going fine; that is until just before the end of the parade. One of the old cars up ahead had stalled in the middle of the road. Gradually everyone had stopped.

Christa and Gypsy pulled up right behind some clowns, who were still carrying on, as clowns do. Gypsy would have been fine, too, if it were not for Mrs. Conley's dress. You see Mrs. Conley was standing right next to the road, beside the very spot, where Gypsy happened to stop. She wore a long flowing red, white, and blue silk dress. She bought it just last week at a department store in the city, just for the parade. And she was very proud of that dress. But the morning breeze was floating the waves of the dress, right in front of Gypsy's face.

This was more than even a well-behaved goat could endure. He had eaten a dress just like that, one time, out of some lady's laundry basket, which was left unattended on a back porch down on Market Street. A silk dress, you know, is just like candy to a goat. Gypsy was just about ready to take a bite, when something caught his eye. Back behind Mrs. Conley was a fence, built around a small pasture. And walking next to the fence was the most beautiful creature that Gypsy had ever seen.

She was a young female goat, strutting along and occasionally stopping to nibble on selective bits of grass.

She had seen Gypsy first, but she just walked by and pretended not to notice him –, as females will sometimes do.

The stalled car was moved; the parade moved on; the silk dress was forgotten. As Gypsy ambled on down the road toward home, this young lady overran his mind. He turned his head to take one last look at her. She stopped and stood by the fence. This time however, she was looking back at him. Then with a wink, and a flit of her tail, she bounded off.

Chapter Nine

Well Gypsy had learned to rub the latch on his chain against the barn post to unfasten it from his collar. He had not done it yet, because he was content at his new home and didn't want to cause any problems.

"Maybe tonight," he thought to himself, "I'll just drop by for a short visit with that young lady. I can easily jump that little fence she's in. Ha!" He then laughed out loud, "That would be the first time I have ever jumped a fence to get in instead of out."

And so it went with Gypsy the goat. Christa wondered why, sometimes in the morning when she went out to visit before school, his chain would not be fastened, when she knew that she had fastened it the night before. But she made nothing of it.

Bart knew. And he also knew that Gypsy had found a new peace, new friends—and two new families.

The End

The Author

I was born and raised on a farm, in the Caldwell community of Orange County, North Carolina. Along with Mama and Daddy my sister, my brother, and I put in a lot of our time working at home. We raised chickens to sell hatching eggs, grew tobacco, corn, wheat, hay; you name it.

We had a lot of animals at different times. Cattle, almost always a milk cow, hogs, and a horse once. The closest to a Gypsy was a duck named Doodles that I won in a school drawing in the second or third grade. He would chase us kids around the house and bite us if he got the chance.

These days, when I'm not writing, I make my living as a building contractor. I am also a licensed aircraft mechanic. For years I have enjoyed flying airplanes and still get the opportunity now and then. I enjoy playing my guitar and like to start every morning by playing for a while.

Vern Miller

The Illustrator

Marsha Cates Stanley resides in Hillsborough, North Carolina with her husband and two children. Marsha enjoys drawing and painting and is passionate about illustrating children's books. She is pleased to have been a part of *Gypsy the Goat*.

Marsha Stanley

CPSIA information can be obtained at www.ICGtesting.com
Printed in the USA
BVOW10s1548160714

359001BV00005B/2/P

9 781611 530827